Be on the lookout
for banks! Economics is
everywhere!

Pat D.S.

GIO & BANKS

Scarcity, Choices, and Tradeoffs

by Pat Segadelli

"*Mamma mia!*" I moan, as I toss and turn in my bed. The anticipation of packing up and moving tomorrow is making it impossible to sleep. My mom told me to try counting sheep, but every time I close my eyes, I find myself counting all of the toys I have to leave behind.

Tired from being up all night, I load the last box of my toys into
the moving van, while giving my best friend Charlie a sad look.

"It won't be that bad," Charlie says.
"I don't know. I have a pit in my stomach the size of Italy!
I've never lived anywhere but this house. I have a feeling New York City
will be nothing like Shoreline."

"C'mon, Gio. Time to hit the road! *Pronti!*" my dad shouts. I give one last secret handshake to Charlie, and slowly walk towards the moving van.

"Goodbye, Gio!" Charlie yells from the sidewalk.
"I'll miss you. Come back and visit soon."
I roll down my window and yell "*ciao*" to Charlie,
our neighborhood, and our house.

My mom's new job in New York means we have to move.
One thing I know for sure is how much I am going to miss this place.

After driving for an eternity, we pull up to a building so tall
that I swear it's high-fiving the sky.
"Let's get unloaded before the truck gets towed," my dad says.
"Our apartment is on the 12th floor."

When I see the apartment, I can't believe my eyes.
The whole place is about as big as our living room back in Shoreline.
I can't believe I had to leave my basketball hoop behind for this.
This move is ruining my life.

The following morning I wake up bright and early.
"*Buongiorno!*" My mom says. "Good morning! What do you want to do today?
You can choose anything."
First I have to choose what toys to bring and now what to do with my first day of
summer break. This is too many choices for an eight year old.

Seeing the disappointment in my eyes, my mom says,
"Why don't you come to work with me today so that I can show you
a little more of the city. C'mon, Gio . . . we'll have fun."

We step out of our high-rise apartment and walk down some stairs into the subway. I had seen pictures of a subway before, but riding on one is way different. I am packed in the train like crayons in my crayon box as it zips and zooms through the underground tunnels.

My mom works on Wall Street. She calls it the financial capital of the world, which means money flows through these streets like water on the Hudson River.

The loud noises hurt my ears. It is enough to turn my brain into scrambled eggs. Everybody is talking on their phones and seems to be in a big hurry.

When I arrive at my mom's office building I look across the street
and I see something I thought you could only see in a zoo.
"Hey Mom! What's that bear doing on Wall Street?"
But Mom seems to be in as much of a hurry as anyone.

We step into the elevator, ready to head up to her office.
How many people could possibly fit in here?
With my head buried in someone else's stomach,
the doors close, and we shoot up like a rocket.

My mom's office is as busy as the sidewalk outside.
Phones ring all the time. And the lights glowing from everybody's
computer screens remind me of Shoreline on Christmas Eve.
I hear words like *dividends, profit margin, and short selling.*
This day is going to be long and boring.

Lunchtime finally arrives, and my mom and I walk to the pizza stand right outside the building to get something to eat.
"You've never had pizza like this before, Gio. New York pizza is the best."
She hands me some money as her phone rings.

As I wait in line, I can't help fixing my eyes on that same bear across the street. My imagination begins to run wild. Am I dreaming? Suddenly, the man behind the pizza stand shouts, "NEXT!" so loud it startles me.

I want a slice of pizza, a cookie, and a soda, but that costs more money than my mom gave me. Ugggh . . . looks like I need to make another choice.
What should I order?

"I'll take a slice of pizza and a soda, please," I tell the man behind the counter. We take our food and decide to eat lunch in the park across the street.

As my mom continues her phone call, I slowly approach the bear.
"Hello . . . ?" I say cautiously.
The bear peers over at me. "You can see me?" he replies.
"Well of course I can see you! Why wouldn't I be able to?" I exclaim.

The bear says, "Nobody's ever talked to me before. Nobody can see me because bears aren't welcome on Wall Street. All anybody around here talks about is that old bull."

"Well my name's Gio." I introduce myself.
"My name is Banks," replies the bear.
"I'm sorry that nobody has ever talked to you before. I know the feeling!
Do you mind if I sit down and eat my lunch?"

My mom was right. New York Pizza is different. The slices are so big
you have to fold them in half just to eat them. I need two hands!
As I dig into my slice, I tell Banks about my big move.

"And the worst part is, my parents said we don't have enough room in our new apartment for all my toys, so I had to leave my mini basketball hoop behind."

"Yeah, sounds like your classic scarcity problem," Banks explains.
"Scare-City? That was the name of the haunted house we would go to
every Halloween back in Shoreline!" I say with excitement.

"No no, not Scare-City. Scarcity. It means the space in your apartment is
limited. You want to bring everything, but there's not enough room for all of it."
As I look up at the sun starting to shine, I can't help but feel I might have a friend
here after all.

"You sound like all the people my mom works with. How do you
know all this?" I ask Banks as I continue to devour my lunch.
"Well," he says, "when you spend your whole life on
Wall Street, you learn a thing or two about economics."
"Economics? Sounds pretty dismal," I respond.

"Gio, economics is AWESOME! Economics is all about scarcity.
Everything is scarce. It's limited. Everything from the space in your apartment,
to the money in your wallet. Even things like the amount of time you have
in your day," Banks explains.

"Just look around this park, Gio. Everything is scarce, and everyone is having to make choices. What choices do you see?" Banks asks.

"Well, that girl only has one cup of lemonade, and she's choosing to share it with her friend. And that man clearly doesn't have enough time, so he's choosing to run through the park. And look at that bird! Even she is having to make a choice!"

"Is there anything that's unlimited?" I question.
"There's just one thing. All of your wants, everything you would have if you could - that's unlimited," Banks explains.

"Economics affects all of us, including you, every day. Because everything is scarce, you have had to make choices. You had to choose what toys to bring and leave behind, how you were going to spend your first day of summer, and whether to get a cookie or a soda."

"So economics is about scarcity and choices?"
"Yep!" Banks responds. "And sacrifices . . . the mini basketball hoop you couldn't bring with you when you moved; the cookie you couldn't have at lunch...those are your tradeoffs - what you had to give up."

"This is all so interesting, but my mom and I need to head back to the office. *Grazie mille*," I say to thank my new friend.
"*Prego!*" He says with a wink. "You're welcome!"
"See you next time?" I hope.
"Only if you choose to visit me again," Banks says grinning. "*Ciao!*"

As the day ends, we get back onto the subway, and I begin thinking of everything Banks taught me. He is right, everything in my life is scarce. I make a million choices every single day. What to have for breakfast, what I am going to play at recess, how I am going to spend my time after school, and what book to read before bed. And every choice means there is something that I have to give up. A tradeoff!

Later, when we arrive home, Dad already has my favorite meal on the table.
"Lasagne!"
"How was your day, Gio?" he asks.
"The best!! I met a bear named Banks, and he explained all sorts of things! Like how because everything is scarce, we are forced to make choices, and those choices all come with tradeoffs!"

"Such a curious mind," my dad chuckles,
while throwing a questionable look at my mom.
She simply shrugs her shoulders.

You know what? Maybe New York City won't be so bad after all.
I met a new friend and learned some cool things. I can't wait to see
what adventure tomorrow will bring.

I look around the table, raise my glass of milk so to cheers my family,
and exclaim, *"Mangiamo!"* "Let's eat!"